Little Sister

Jump Rope Rhymes

THIS BOOK BELONGS TO

_____

Look for these and other books about Karen in the Baby-sitters Little Sister series:

Little Sister

Jump Rope Rhymes

ANN M. MARTIN

A
LITTLE **APPLE**
PAPERBACK

SCHOLASTIC INC.
New York Toronto London Auckland Sydney

*The author gratefully acknowledges
Nancy E. Krulik for her help
with this book.*

Cover art by Susan Tang
Interior art by John DeVore

ISBN 0-590-25995-4

Copyright © 1995 by Ann M. Martin.
All rights reserved. Published by Scholastic Inc.
APPLE PAPERBACKS and BABY-SITTERS LITTLE SISTER
are registered trademarks of Scholastic Inc.

12 11 10 9 8 7 6 5 4   5 6 7 8 9/9 0/0

Printed in the U.S.A.   40

First Scholastic printing, July 1995

Jumpin' Jimminy!

If you love jumping rope (like Karen, Nancy, and Hannie do) then you have come to the right place. This book is filled with fun jump rope rhymes to say while you skip rope. Some you can say while jumping with your brand-new Baby-sitters Little Sister jump rope. Others are for you and your pals to try while using one (or even two) extra-long jump ropes.

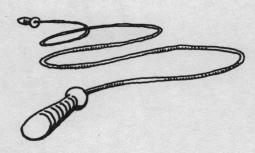

You may know some of the rhymes in this book. Others will be new to you. Some are special rhymes made up by Karen and her pals. When you say those rhymes you can insert the names of *your* friends and family instead of the names of the kids from Stoneybrook.

Happy jumping!

Left Foot, Right Foot

Left foot
Right foot
Left foot
Right
Karen jumps all day and night.
Left foot
Right foot
Left foot down
Jumping rope all over town!

When you jump rope to this rhyme, be sure to land on only one foot at a time. When you say the word "left," hop on your left foot. When you say the word "right," hop on your right foot.

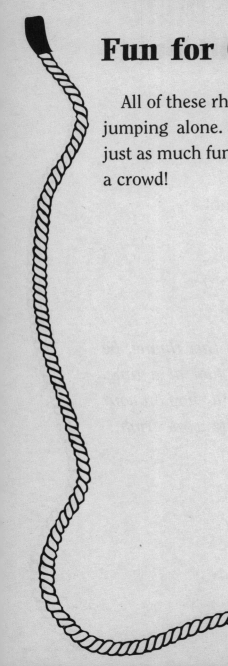

Fun for One!

All of these rhymes can be said by anyone jumping alone. But guess what. They are just as much fun when you're jumping with a crowd!

Karen's First Rhyme

This is the first jump rope rhyme Karen ever learned, back when she wasn't much older than Andrew. Here's what you do: Swing the rope back and forth on the ground and jump over it. When you get to the word "over" turn the rope over your head and start jumping rope.

Silver bells
Cockleshells
Eevy, ivy OVER!

It's Pickling Time!

Here's a recipe to spice up any of the rhymes in this book: Start with this little poem. Then add your favorite rhyme, and jump!

Late last night
Or the night before
A nickel and pickle
Came knocking on my door,
And this is what they said . . .

Now add your favorite rhyme.

Cinderella Stories

Emily Michelle loves the story of Cinderella. She also loves Karen's Cinderella jump rope rhymes. Here are six of Emily's favorites. See if you can come up with any of your own.

Cinderella
Dressed in yellow
Went upstairs to kiss her fellow.
How many kisses did she get?
One, two, three, four, five, six . . .

Keep going until you miss.

Cinderella
Dressed in lace
Went upstairs to fix her face.
How many powder puffs did it take?
One, two, three, four, five, six . . .

Cinderella
Dressed in silk
Went outside to get some milk.
How many cows did she find?
One, two, three, four, five, six . . .

Cinderella
Dressed in bows
Went downstairs to blow her nose.
How many tissues did it take?
One, two, three, four, five, six . . .

Cinderella
Dressed in blue.
Prince looked down and found her shoe.
How many bridesmaids did they have?
One, two, three, four, five, six . . .

Cinderella
Dressed in yellow.
By mistake she kissed a snake
How many doctors did it take?
One, two, three, four, five, six . . .

Three Best Friends

Hannie and Nancy went to town
Hannie bought an evening gown.
Nancy bought a pair of shoes,
Karen watched the evening news.
And this is what it said . . .
One, two, three, four, five, six . . .

Berry Yummy!

Nannie, Nannie
Baked a pie.
How many berries did she buy?
One, two, three, four, five, six . . .

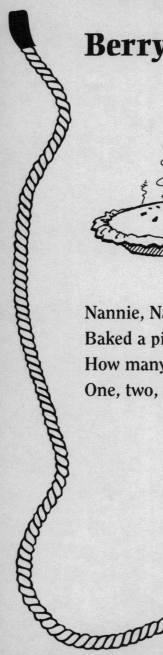

Spinach Sayings!

Popeye went to the cellar
To drink some spinach juice.
How many gallons did he drink?
One, two, three, four, five, six . . .

What a Bellyache!

Karen looked near and far,
Then she snuck some cookies
from the cookie jar.
How many cookies did it take
Before she had a bellyache?
One, two, three, four, five, six . . .

Happy Birthday!

Happy birthday
To you, to you.
Tell me, tell me, tell me true
How old, how old, how old are you?
One, two, three, four, five, six . . .

Counting Calendar

Snowballs in the winter
Each summer we hike.
Tell me which season do you like?
January, February, March, April . . .

Baseball Fever!

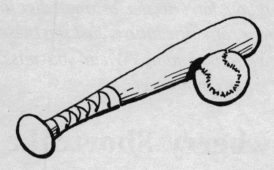

*Karen wrote this rhyme especially for her
big sister—and softball coach—Kristy!*

Kristy's Krushers is our name
Playing softball is our game!
Running the bases is our chore.
How many runs can we score?
One, two, three, four, five, six . . .

True Love?

There was a fortune-teller at Karen's carnival. But you don't need a fortune-teller to predict your romantic future. Just say these rhymes while you jump. When you miss, you will know your answer.

Strawberry Shortcake

Strawberry shortcake
Cream on top.
Tell me the name of your sweetheart.
Is it A, B, C, D . . .

When you miss, you have to come up with a boy's name that starts with that letter. Sometimes Karen misses on purpose when she reaches R. After all, Ricky Torres is her pretend husband!

Hannie Loves Scott

Hannie, Hannie tell me true.
You love Scott, but does he love you?
Yes, no, yes, no, yes . . .

Flower Power!

Daisy, daisy
Special flower
Will my love be here this hour?
Yes, no, maybe so. Yes, no, maybe so . . .

The Wedding

Will I marry?
Yes, no, yes, no . . .

Who will I marry?
A, B, C, D, E . . .

Where will we marry?
Church, synagogue, field, house, barn,
Church, synagogue, field, house, barn . . .

How many children will we have?
One, two, three, four, five, six . . .

Three "Three Musketeers" Rhymes

These are rhymes about everyone's favorite pals — Karen, Hannie, and Nancy! Do you have special friends you would like to sing about?

She's not a blushing beauty
With cheeks like a rose
She's just your pal Karen,
With freckles on her nose.

Hannie loves Bip
Nancy loves Bop
The Musketeers love each other
Like a pig loves slop!

They may be rich,
They may be poor.
But the Three Musketeers
Are friends ever more!

Here Comes the Ice Cream Truck!

These three rhymes are summer treats!

I scream
You scream
We all scream for ice cream!

I says
You says
We all want ices!

Jump around in a circle when you say this rhyme.

Cherry ices
Five cents a lick
When I spin around,
It makes me sick!

Boy oh Boy!

Two rhymes all about boys.

I like coffee, I like tea.
I like the boys and the boys like me!

Mother, mother, mother
Pin a rose on me.
All the boys are stuck on me!

K-I-S-S and Tell!

Karen is a champion speller. She likes this rhyme because she gets to spell out a word.

Karen and Ricky sitting in a tree.
K-I-S-S-I-N-G
First comes love
Then comes marriage.
Next comes a baby in the baby carriage.
Sucking his thumb.
Wetting his pants.
Doing a hula bula dance.

Remember, you can replace Karen's and Ricky's names with your friends' names.

Morbidda Destiny's Cat

When Karen first learned this game she called it the Witch's Cat. But since she is certain her next-door neighbor is really a witch named Morbidda Destiny, Karen changed the name of the game. To play the game you must jump rope while you say this alphabet rhyme:

Morbidda's cat
Is an Awesome cat
And its name is Alison.

Morbidda's cat
Is a Beautiful cat
And its name is Bethany.

Morbidda's cat
Is a Cool cat
And its name is Cathy . . .

Keep going until you step on the rope or you can't think of a word or name.

A special hint from Karen: X is a really tough letter. So, as a special treat, Karen has decided to tell you her secret X rhyme.

Morbidda's cat is a Xanthic cat
And its name is Xavier!

(Xanthic means yellow in color. You pronounce it "zanthic.")

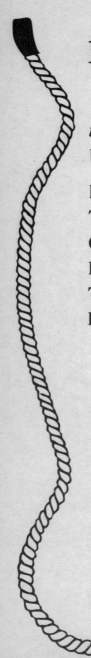

Hello Miss

There's no miss-stake! When you say these rhymes, you're supposed to miss! Wait for the word "Miss," though.

Karen's waiting at
The garden gate.
Once again
I'm running late.
Two, four, six, eight
Here I am, MISS!

I have a brother
We call mister.
I have a sister
We call MISS!

Miss, miss, little miss.
When she misses,
She misses like this . . . MISS!

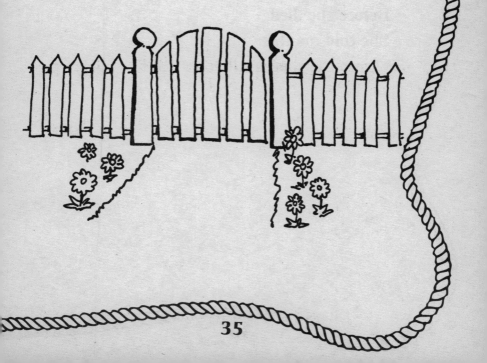

Lisa, Lisa, she likes kisses!
She met Seth.
Made her a Mrs.
No more MISS!

Little Mary Lou
Dressed in blue
Died last night
At half past two.
Before she died
She told me this:
"Jump the rope until you MISS!"

Pass the Pepper

How fast can you jump? Find out. When you say the word "pepper" speed up!

Pass the salt
And the ketchup, please.
Forget the PEPPER!
It makes me sneeze.
Aaachoo!

Add some spices
To my supper.
Remember the salt
And the super PEPPER upper!

Kristy went off to the store.
This is what she went there for:
Coffee, tea, bread, and PEPPER!

Up and down the ladder wall,
Penny loaf to feed us all.
I'll buy the milk
You get the flour,
Karen brings the PEPPER in half an hour.

Mabel, Mabel
Set the table.
Don't forget the salt and PEPPER!

Michael Finnegan

This rhyme is really an old camp song Karen learned at Camp Mohawk.

I knew a man named Michael Finnegan
He had whiskers on his chinnegan.
Along came the wind and blew them in
    again.
Poor old Michael Finnegan.
Begin again.

Rainbow Rhymer!

Black, black, sit on a tack.
Brown, brown, you're a clown.
Green, green, a fairy queen.
Red, red, stay in bed.
White, white, go fly a kite.
Yellow, yellow, loves her fellow!

Can you come up with any other colorful rhymes?

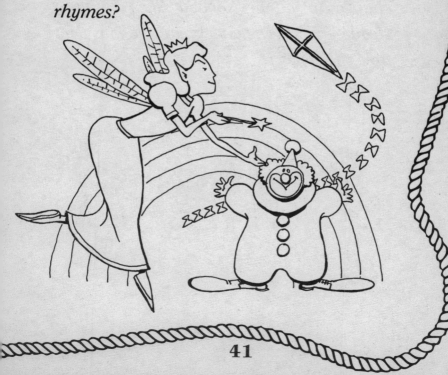

Rhymes for Three Musketeers or More!

Having the crowd over to jump rope? Why not try some of these fun rhymes? With each rhyme you'll find instructions to tell you what to do while you're jumping. But be careful — sometimes they can be tricky. And be sure you give everyone a chance to jump. Nobody likes being a steady ender! (The enders are the kids who turn the ropes.)

Hurry, hurry don't be late.

Meet us at the garden gate.

(Jump in)

Jump it high!

(Enders raise the rope high off the ground)

Jump it low!

(Enders lower the rope so the jumper must crouch to jump)

Turn around

(Jump in a circle)

And out you go!

(Run out)

The Sea-soned Sailor

This jump rope rhyme is really old! Karen was amazed to learn that Kristy had jumped to it when she was Karen's age. But imagine Karen's surprise when she learned that her stepmother, Elizabeth, had jumped to it, too! Someday, even Emily will probably be saying the sailor rhyme. But let's wait until she's talking!

When you hear the word see or sea, put your hand above your eyes like a salute. When you hear the name of a body part, touch that part while you are jumping.

A sailor went to sea sea sea
To see what he could see, see, see.
But all that he could see, see, see
Was the bottom of the deep blue
    sea, sea, sea.

A sailor went to nose, nose, nose
To nose what he could nose, nose, nose.

But all that he could nose, nose, nose
Was the bottom of the deep blue nose,
   nose, nose.

A sailor went to elbow, elbow, elbow
To elbow what he could elbow, elbow,
   elbow.
But all that he could elbow, elbow, elbow
Was the bottom of the deep blue elbow,
   elbow, elbow.

A sailor went to knee, knee, knee
To knee what he could knee, knee, knee.
But all that he could knee, knee, knee
Was the bottom of the deep blue knee,
   knee, knee.

Silly Sally Water

This silly rhyme will keep you moving!

Silly Sally Water
Sitting in a saucer *(Bend down)*
Rise Sally rise *(Stand up)*
Dry your eyes *(Close your eyes)*
Put your hand on your hip *(Place your
    hand on your hip)*
Don't let your backbone slip
Turn to the east *(Turn right)*
Turn to the west *(Turn left)*
Point to the kid that you like best!
    *(Point to the person who should jump in
    next. Then you jump out!)*

Teddy Bear, Teddy Bear

Since Karen is a two-two, she loves this doubly fun beary *tricky rhyme!*

Teddy bear, teddy bear
Turn around.
   (Jump in a circle)
Teddy bear, teddy bear
Touch the ground.
   (Bend down and touch the ground)
Teddy bear, teddy bear
Tie your shoe.
   (Touch your shoe)
Teddy Bear, teddy bear
Point to the sky.
   (Point up)
Teddy bear, teddy bear
Close your eyes.
   (Close your eyes)

Teddy bear, teddy bear
That will do.
Teddy bear, teddy bear
Take your bow.
  (Take a bow)
Teddy bear, teddy bear
Jump out now!
  (Run out)

Beautiful Ballerina

Jessi, a girl in the Baby-sitters Club who wants to be a prima ballerina, taught Hannie this rhyme.

Ballerina in a show
Ballerina point your toe.
   (Jump on tippy-toe)
Ballerina twirl around.
   (Jump in a circle)
Place your palm upon the
   ground.
   (Bend down and touch the ground)
Jump as high as you can go.
   (Jump very high)
Now try it jumping low.
   (Crouch down as you jump)
Ballerina end your show. *(Take a bow)*
Ballerina it's time to go! *(Run out)*

High Up There!

For this rhyme, the enders start with the rope about an inch off the ground. They gradually raise it higher as they say the rhyme over and over and over.

When it rains
The Mississippi River
Gets higher, higher, higher!

Shoo Fly!

Shoo away the fly
   (Wave your hands in the air)
Scratch away the flea
   (Scratch your tummy)
Tickle my foot
   (Touch the sole of your shoe)
And out goes me!
   (Jump out)

Better Butter

Two girls jump at the same time. When they say the word "squeeze," they hug, and then jump out.

Butter is butter
Cheese is cheese.
What is a hug
Without a squeeze?

Time's Up!

It's time for fun! In this rhyme, two girls jump together. Karen is the "clock face" so she jumps straight up and down. Hannie is the "hands of the clock," so she jumps in a circle around Karen.

Tick tock
Tick tock
Karen is a cuckoo clock.
The clock stays still
While the hands go round.
One, two, three, four,
  five, six . . .

When she reaches the number twelve, Hannie jumps out. Now Karen becomes the hands, and Natalie becomes the clock.

In I Run

In I run *(Jump in)*
And around I go. *(Jump in a circle)*
I lift my knee *(Bend one knee)*
And slap my shoe. *(Slap your shoe)*
As I go out *(You jump out)*
Let Hannie come in.
   (The next jumper jumps in)

   Don't forget to use your friend's name in place of Hannie's.

Everybody In!

These rhymes are most fun when you play with lots and lots of jumpers. Ms. Colman's whole class likes to try them at recess. Maybe yours will, too.

Everybody come on in.
The first one to miss
Must take my end!

Five, ten, fifteen, twenty.
Do not leave the jump rope empty!

Knock, Knock

You will need at least five players for this game. Two kids jump at one time. Natalie jumps in first and says:

Knock, knock the doors are calling
Calling Karen to the door.
   (Karen jumps in and joins Natalie)
Now Karen is the one
Who's having all the fun
And we don't need Natalie anymore.
   (Natalie jumps out)

Knock, knock the doors are calling
Calling Hannie to the door.
   (Hannie jumps in and joins Karen)
Now Hannie is the one
Who's having all the fun
And we don't need Karen anymore.
   (Karen jumps out)

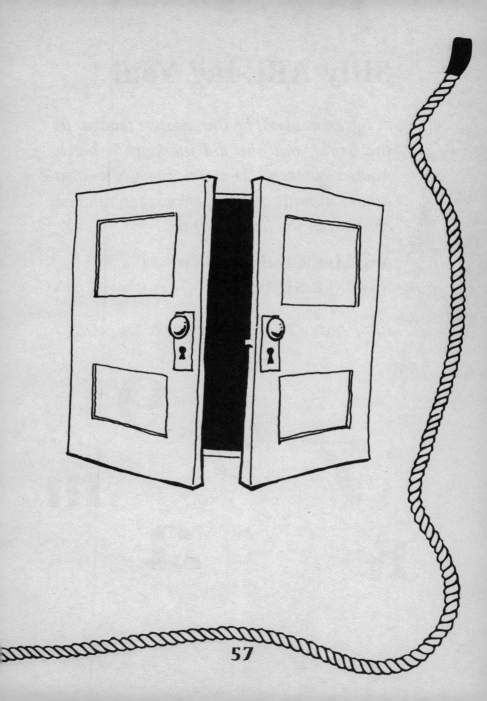

Silly ABC-ing You!

Karen may not be the greatest teacher in the world, but she did manage to teach Andrew to read Hop on Pop. She also taught him his alphabet. Now even Andrew can join in the jump rope fun!

A B C D E F G H I J K L M
N O P Q R S T U are out!

Jump out of the rope when you say "out."

7 3 9 m R a

Rattlesnake

The enders crouch down on their knees and wriggle the rope back and forth on the ground. The jumper has to jump back and forth over the wriggling rope. Sound easy? It's not. That's because the enders must keep wiggling the rope faster and faster. You know what happens when you step on a rattlesnake? You have to take an end, that's what! While you play, say this over and over again:

R-A-T-T-L-E-S-N-A-K-E spells rattlesnake!

Low Rent Rhyme!

Now here's a switch — this rhyme is about one of the enders. In this case, that's Hannie. When the rhyme is through, the jumper takes Hannie's end.

Hannie, Hannie lived in a tent
To the landlord she paid no rent.
She borrowed one
She borrowed two
She passed the end along to you!

Catch the Fox!

Get ready for a fox hunt! You will need lots of kids to play this game: two to take the ends, one to be the fox, and lots of others to be chasers! The enders stand and swing the rope back and forth on the ground. The "fox" jumps back and forth over the rope and says:

Catch the fox . . . Karen! *(or anyone else who happens to be playing).*

Then the chase is on! The players must run in a figure eight, going around the enders and over the rope until the "chaser" catches the "fox." Once the "fox" is tagged, the "chaser" becomes the "fox" and gets to choose who chases.

Double Dutch!

Double the ropes! Double the jumps! Double the fun!

Double Dutch is a jump rope game that started out in cities across America. Now you can join the double Dutch crowd. We'll show you how!

When you jump double Dutch you use two ropes. The enders turn the ropes in opposite directions making sure that at any given time, one rope is in the air, and one is sweeping against the ground. You have to be very careful not to turn the ropes in the same direction or so that they are both in the air at the same time. That's called double ending, and it makes it almost impossible for the jumper to jump.

Jumping double Dutch is tough. Since there are two ropes, you have to make twice as many jumps. It's easiest to jump from one foot to another instead of jumping on two feet at one time.

Remember, it might take you a very long time to learn to turn and jump double Dutch. In fact, Kristy told Karen that some of the Baby-sitters Club members still have trouble jumping double (and they've been doing it for years!).

Double Dutch Rhymes

Jumping double Dutch is so tough that some kids don't even like to say rhymes while they are jumping — they'd rather concentrate on those two ropes. If that's how you and your pals feel, why not ask the enders to cheer the jumper on. All they have to do is say "go," over and over again. For instance, Nancy and Hannie might say:

"Go Karen! Go Karen! Go Karen!"

But once you've mastered the double Dutch jump, you'll want to get your tongue ready for some doubly quick rhymes!

Right! Left!

Here are the rules: Make sure your right foot hits the ground when you say "right," and your left foot hits the ground when you say "left."

Left! Right!

I left my wife and 22 children alone in the house without any cake. Did I do right? No, I left. Left. Left my wife and 22 kids alone in the house without any cake. Left! Right! I left my wife and 22 children . . .

Boo Boo's Boo-Boo

There's music in a hammer.
There's music in a nail.
There's music in a Boo-Boo.
Until you step upon his tail!

Red Hot!

One rope is on the bottom
The other's on the top.
When I say "hot" go faster,
And when I miss you stop!
HOT!

When the jumper says the word "hot,"
turn the ropes as fast as pepper!

Write on Rhyme Pages

Have we missed any of your favorite rhymes? Have you decided to be creative and make up a few rockin' rhymes of your own? No jump rope book would be complete if it left out any of the rhymes you and your friends like to jump to. That's why Karen and the gang have left you some space to write down even more jump rope rhymes. So put down the rope (for a little while anyway) and take out your pencil.

_____

_____

_____

_____

_____

_____

_____

9

12

7 3

R

Little Sister™

by Ann M. Martin, author of *The Baby-sitters Club*®

More Titles... ➡

The Baby-sitters Little Sister titles continued...

❑ MQ44825-0	#29	Karen's Cartwheel	$2.75
❑ MQ45645-8	#30	Karen's Kittens	$2.75
❑ MQ45646-6	#31	Karen's Bully	$2.95
❑ MQ45647-4	#32	Karen's Pumpkin Patch	$2.95
❑ MQ45648-2	#33	Karen's Secret	$2.95
❑ MQ45650-4	#34	Karen's Snow Day	$2.95
❑ MQ45652-0	#35	Karen's Doll Hospital	$2.95
❑ MQ45651-2	#36	Karen's New Friend	$2.95
❑ MQ45653-9	#37	Karen's Tuba	$2.95
❑ MQ45655-5	#38	Karen's Big Lie	$2.95
❑ MQ45654-7	#39	Karen's Wedding	$2.95
❑ MQ47040-X	#40	Karen's Newspaper	$2.95
❑ MQ47041-8	#41	Karen's School	$2.95
❑ MQ47042-6	#42	Karen's Pizza Party	$2.95
❑ MQ46912-6	#43	Karen's Toothache	$2.95
❑ MQ47043-4	#44	Karen's Big Weekend	$2.95
❑ MQ47044-2	#45	Karen's Twin	$2.95
❑ MQ47045-0	#46	Karen's Baby-sitter	$2.95
❑ MQ43647-3		Karen's Wish Super Special #1	$2.95
❑ MQ44834-X		Karen's Plane Trip Super Special #2	$3.25
❑ MQ44827-7		Karen's Mystery Super Special #3	$2.95
❑ MQ45644-X		Karen's Three Musketeers Super Special #4	$2.95
❑ MQ45649-0		Karen's Baby Super Special #5	$3.25
❑ MQ46911-8		Karen's Campout Super Special #6	$3.25

Available wherever you buy books, or use this order form.

Scholastic Inc., P.O. Box 7502, 2931 E. McCarty Street, Jefferson City, MO 65102

Please send me the books I have checked above. I am enclosing $ _____
(please add $2.00 to cover shipping and handling). Send check or money order - no cash
or C.O.Ds please.

Name _____ Birthdate_____

Address _____

City _____ State/Zip_____

Please allow four to six weeks for delivery. Offer good in U.S.A. only. Sorry, mail orders are not
available to residents to Canada. Prices subject to change.   BLS793

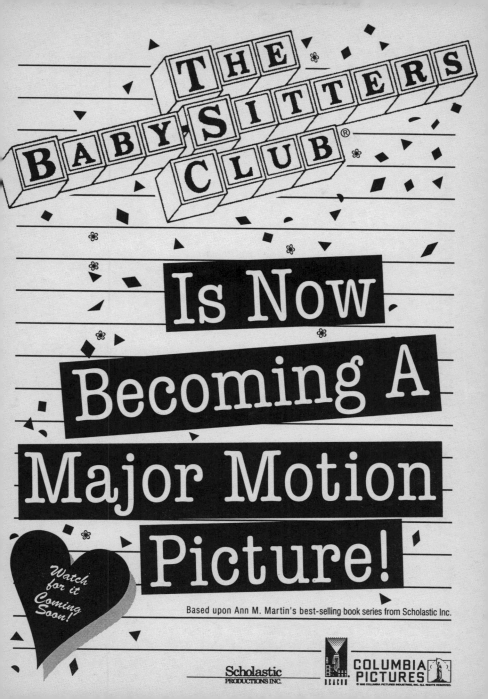

Coming to theaters this summer!

THE BABY-SITTERS CLUB® MOVIE

Big things are happening in Stoneybrook
and the cameras are rolling....
It's a major motion picture based on your
favorite books and starring your
favorite baby-sitters!

**And don't miss this!
Look for four all-new, never-before-
published BSC books based on
the big screen adventures of
The Baby-sitters Club Movie, and
jam-packed with plenty of
photos from the film.**

Tell your friends about **The Baby-sitters Club Movie.**
Opens nationwide this summer.

BSCM1194